Am i THE PRiNCESS
OR THE FROG?

Think you can handle *another* Jamie Kelly diary?

#1 LET'S PRETEND THIS NEVER HAPPENED

#2 MY PANTS ARE HAUNTED!

#3 AM I THE PRINCESS OR THE FROG?

#4 NEVER DO ANYTHING, EVER

#5 CAN ADULTS BECOME HUMAN?

#6 THE PROBLEM WITH HERE IS THAT IT'S WHERE I'M FROM

#7 NEVER UNDERESTIMATE YOUR DUMBNESS

#8 IT'S NOT MY FAULT I KNOW EVERYTHING

#9 THAT'S WHAT FRIENDS AREN'T FOR

#10 THE WORST THINGS IN LIFE ARE ALSO FREE

#11 OKAY, SO MAYBE I DO HAVE SUPERPOWERS

#12 ME! (JUST LIKE YOU, ONLY BETTER)

AND DON'T MISS . . .

DEAR DUMB DIARY YEAR TWO #1:
SCHOOL. HASN'T THIS GONE ON LONG ENOUGH?

Jim Benton's Tales from Mackerel Middle School

DEAR DUMB DIARY,

AM I THE PRINCESS OR THE FROG?

SCHOLASTIC INC.
New York Toronto London Auckland
Sydney Mexico City New Delhi Hong Kong

ISBN 978-0-545-44342-5

12 11 10 9 8 7 6 5 4 3 2 1 12 13 14 15 16 17/0

Printed in the U.S.A. 40

This edition first printing, February 2012

For All Good Dogs, and in particular a few that have trotted down the trail ahead of us: Max, Truffles, Josette, Max, Mimi, Billy, Sadie, and Henry.

Special thanks to:
Maria Barbo, Steve Scott, Susan Jeffers Casel, and Shannon Penney.

THIS DIARY PROPERTY OF

Jamie Kelly

SCHOOL: Mackerel Middle School

Locker: 101

Best friend: Isabella

Destiny: Princess OR Spy/Ballerina

Pet: Beagle-shaped thing

GREAT DANGER AWAITS
YE WHO READS FURTHER.

I'm serious. Thou shalt be **CURSED** if thou reads further. And you can tell I'm serious because it says SHALT and thou.

She means it

Dear Whoever Is Reading My Dumb Diary,

Are you sure you're supposed to be reading somebody else's diary? Have you done this before? If I did **NOT** give you permission, you had better stop right **NOW**.

If you are my parents, then **YES**, I know that I am not allowed to call people idiots and fools and turds and trolls and all that, but this is a diary, and I didn't actually "call" them anything. I ***wrote*** it. And, if you punish me for it, then I will know that you read my diary, which you do ***not*** have permission to do.

Now, by the power vested in me, I do promise that everything in this diary is true, or at least as true as I think it needs to be.

Signed,

Jamie Kelly

PS: Although if it's **You-know-who** that's reading my diary, well, then, it's totally okay. But if it's **You-know-who,** then you had better close this book right now, or else **You-know-who** is going to get a **you-know-what** in the **you-know-where.** You know?

PPS: I know that you don't believe in fairies or anything, so you probably wouldn't believe a fairy could turn you into a frog if you kept reading. But I'll bet you believe in hammers and I'll bet you believe that I have one and I'll bet you believe that I know where your head is. Let's just say that fairies are not your biggest worry if you decide to keep reading.

Saturday 31

Isabella was over for most of the day today and we worked out our entire future together. We're going to marry identical twins and live next door to each other and have exactly the same number of kids (nine girls, eight boys) and we'll time it so that they're all the same ages as each other's kids.

We'll have our own clothing store but we won't sell anything good to people we hate. Our husbands will be firemen or doctors or something, but they have to be the same thing so that neither one of us is richer than the other. And if one of our husbands gets in an accident and loses a foot or something, the other husband will have to cut his off just to be fair.

I really didn't think this was a reasonable thing to expect from a husband, especially if instead of getting a foot cut off it's something like falling out of an airplane. But Isabella says that she is much more of an expert on guys than I am, and that our husbands will be so totally into us that they will probably come up with this idea by themselves, anyway.

Sunday 01

Dear Dumb Diary,

Once again, Mom committed **Dinner** against the entire family tonight. As usual, I'm up here in my room clutching my guts wondering what the police would call this particular food crime. Maybe **Assault with a Breaded Weapon**? Or **Hamicide**?

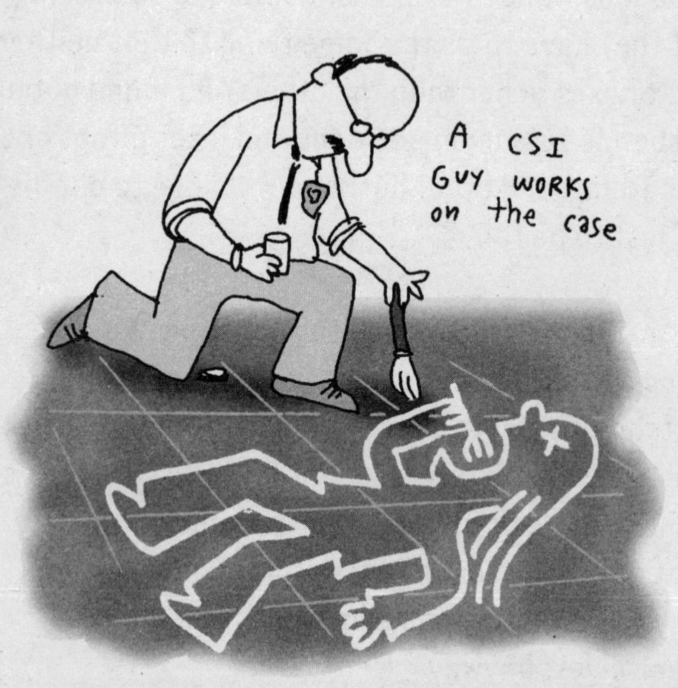
A CSI GUY WORKS on the case

I really don't know what kind of meat was in the **Meat Thing,** but I'm sure that Mom has a cookbook somewhere called ***101 Recipes Using Ingredients That Shun the Daylight.***

Dad and I have been trying not to complain about the food because a few weeks ago, Mom had one of her Nobody-Appreciates-How-Hard-It-Is-to-Make-Dinner-and-One-Day-You'll-Appreciate-My-Cooking episodes. In retrospect, Dad and I probably should not have held our noses all the way through dinner.

Fortunately, I had the foresight to make a candy necklace out of Rolaids, so I can kind of medicate myself throughout the meals. Dad's not so lucky.

Mom might notice if Dad wore a Big Honking Necklace to Dinner

WARNING TO MY FUTURE CHILDREN: If I ever have children and they are reading my diary right now, I want you to know, kids, that you must never ever ever eat Grandma's cooking. Also, My Little Darlings, you are grounded for reading my diary, so go find Mommy right now and tell her what you've done, because you're in for a HUGE punishment.

And I'm telling Santa.

Children! Beware of Grandma's Baked Uck!

Since it's Sunday, Dumb Diary, I have to work on the homework that's due tomorrow instead of sitting on the couch watching reruns of reality TV shows, which is what I'd really like to be doing. As Dad helpfully pointed out, if I had finished my h.w. on Friday, I could be relaxing right now. Dads are really good at pointing out *Things Everybody Already Knew.*

Anyway, we're finishing up our poetry unit in English class right now, and I have to write a poem about feelings. Here's what I have so far:

Mother dear, you've helped me grow
Into a pretty blossom.
So now I'd really like to know
Why you would feed me possum.

Monday 02

Dear Dumb Diary,

Angeline rears her ugly head! Which of course isn't ugly, and I'm not even going to talk about her rears. You get the idea.

You remember last week how I told you that Isabella told me that Anika Martin, who is friends with Amy Feinstein (who we talk to sometimes even though she was born with the handicap of being a year younger than us), who is friends with a girl named Vanessa Something, who knows Angeline's cousin, told *her* that she had heard that Angeline had come up with a new top secret shampooing technique.

Supposedly, Angeline has invented something called **ZONE SHAMPOOING.** The idea is that you shampoo each zone of your head with its own distinct fragrance of shampoo. Anytime Angeline wants to, she can flip her hair in one direction or the other and shoot a delicious waft of fragrance right at your unsuspecting nose. More diabolical yet, she can sequence her hair flips and combine fragrances so that maybe you think you just smelled apple pie with vanilla cinnamon ice cream, or maybe a kiwi-strawberry smoothie with a touch of key lime.

Why would somebody want to do this evil thing?

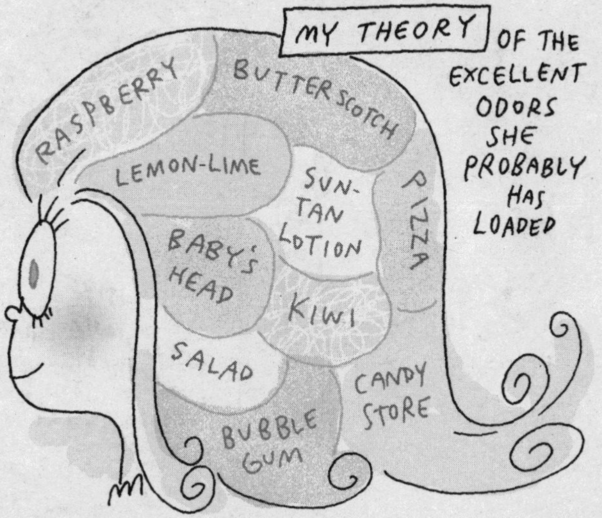

Well, Dumb Diary, I can tell you why somebody might **NOT** want to do this thing. Today I gave Zone Shampooing a try, and when I attempted to shoot Hudson Rivers (eighth-cutest boy in my grade) a snootful of Raspberry Delight (right side of head) combined with Coconut Madness (left lower quadrant of head), my English teacher, Mr. Evans—who was walking by at that exact moment—saw my attempt and thought I was having a seizure. He took me to the office, and the school nurse made me lie down on the cot for a while.

WHIP
WHIP
FLAIL
WHIP
seriously—why would somebody think this was a seizure?

Then, at lunch, Isabella admitted that maybe she didn't have the story straight and might have made some of it up. I don't really blame her, though — it sounds so much like something Angeline might do that if I had made it up myself, I probably would have believed it, too.

Other things Isabella can't remember if she really heard or just made up.

You can play a slice of Baloney in a DVD player.

Some perfume has whale Vomit in it.

Here, we throw rice at weddings. In Japan, they throw hamburgers.

It is medically impossible to put on mascara with your mouth shut.

Tuesday 03

Dear Dumb Diary,

I was the first person who had to read my poem out loud in Mr. Evans's class today. He liked it, I think, and he said something about something and then something else about something else, and I think he might have continued on about something else after that for a while, finishing up with something about something. I know that I am supposed to be paying better attention to Mr. Evans, but I was trying to watch Angeline out of the corner of my eye and didn't hear everything Mr. Evans said.

I was trying to watch Hudson at the same time out of the corner of my other eye, which, in fairness to Mr. Evans, probably **DID** look a little bit like I was having another seizure — kind of like the one I didn't have yesterday — and I was sent down to the office again for a little lie-down time on the cot.

Even though Mr. Evans was pretty sure I was going mental, he still made sure that I caught the next big assignment on the way out the door. Now that we're done with poetry, we have to select a popular fairy tale and write a report about it.

See, some teachers don't care if you're sick — they still make you do your work. I heard that one time this kid had one of his legs chopped off by a snow blower on the way to school, but since he had Mr. Evans, the kid dragged himself to school anyway, and Mr. Evans is so strict that he marked the kid *partially* absent.

FAIRY TALE ASSIGNMENT
1. PICK A FAIRY TALE.
2. HOW DOES IT APPLY TO YOUR LIFE?
3. I DON'T CARE IF YOU'RE DEAD. DO IT ANYWAY.

Wednesday 04

Dear Dumb Diary,

As you know, Dumb Diary (since I like to doodle on your face every day), art is one of my favorite subjects. But today in art class, Miss Anderson (the teacher who is pretty enough to be a waitress) said we're going to be doing a project involving photography, which, according to her, is art.

I think that's kind of like saying that recording a song is the same as singing one, but Miss Anderson is one of the few teachers I really really like, so I only performed a mild dirty look when she said it.

Miss Anderson Does not HAve to Be A teacher
She might even be pretty enough to be a shoe salesperson

Had I known that she was going to buddy me up with Angeline on the project, I would have used a much stronger dirty look. Possibly even ***Dirty Look Number Eleven.***

(Note: It's important to practice your dirty looks and keep them numbered. Never try to mix them. Once I detonated numbers 8 and 4 at the same time, and it came out looking like a smile. It's a long story, but that accidental smile is why I unintentionally went with my aunt one time when she needed to shop for her big old bras.)

Our photo projects are going to go up in the lunchroom at the end of the month for the whole school to see. Angeline already had an idea for ours and, before talking it over with me, she just blurted it out in front of the entire class. That's right, Dumb Diary, she just "cuts the idea" the way some people cut farts.

Angeline suggested that she and I collect pictures of all the teachers when they were kids and make a big collage out of them so that everybody can see for themselves, I guess, just how punishing time is on the human body. Miss Anderson loved the idea, of course. As anybody can plainly see, she is beautiful now so she was for sure even more beautiful before she became a teacher (since there is no way that working with kids can improve your appearance).

So she told us to get started.

The woman who worked with kids
Day 1
Day 2

I know what you're thinking, Dumb Diary. You're thinking, ***"Wow, Jamie. You're totally pretty and a really good dancer."*** I'm not going to tell you you're wrong, Dumb Diary, but please, try to stay on the subject. There is more to this whole art class tragedy.

It's true
my grooves
are
righteous

My so-called best friend, Isabella — who may be missing that part of the body where you keep your soul (It might be called the Soul Hole. I'm not a doctor.) — announces that ***her*** photography project is to put up pictures of everyone in the class with their pet, to show how people and their pets look alike.

"PEOPLE AND THEIR PETS LOOK ALIKE," she says.

First off, my pet is a dog, which is the international symbol for **Ugly Girl**, and my dog is the dog that other dogs are grateful that they at least don't look as bad as.

I don't want to say that Stinker is ugly, but the only reason other dogs sniff him is to see which end is his face.

So, thanks a lot, Isabella.

PS: I tried to secretly sniff Angeline from two sides today to see if she really is Zone Shampooing. I couldn't tell the difference. I don't think there is such a thing.

PPS: There is, however, a way to creep somebody out by trying to smell both sides of their head.

Other ways I have creeped people out in the past
Tried to casually peer up Uncle's nose
tasted comb
mmm mmmm
was spotted practicing kissing on arm

Thursday 05

Dear Dumb Diary,

That's right. It's Thursday. And Thursday, at Mackerel Middle School and other penitentiaries, is traditionally **Meat Loaf Day.** That means it's also the day we traditionally get all sorts of grief from Miss Bruntford, the cafeteria monitor, for not finishing our meat loaf.

Today, I quietly mentioned that the people on *Fear Factor* wouldn't finish our meat loaf, either. Evidently, I said it loud enough for Miss Bruntford's houndlike ears to pick it up, because she came right over and said to me, "What? What is so terrible about this meat loaf?"

And then, Dumb Diary, she took a bite.

Okay, here's the thing: I don't hate teachers. I actually like some of them. (One time, I even saw one at the mall and she was buying underwear such as actual people wear.)

But when Miss Bruntford took a bite of the meat loaf, and her mouth was filled with the flavor that many have described as a combination of a petting zoo in July and a burning bag of hair, well, I have to tell you, it was a beautiful, beautiful moment.

I'm not even sure how to describe it exactly. I think Miss Bruntford herself summed it up best when she said . . .

Call
9-1-1!

Friday 06

Dear Dumb Diary,

I'm not sure what happened to Miss Bruntford. She wasn't in school today, and there was something so pleasant about it all that I temporarily forgave Isabella for her stupid people-pet lookalike idea and we ate together at lunch. Isabella says she heard that Miss Bruntford is in the hospital with **Spontaneous Diverticulosis** or something. It's one of those old-people diseases that makes them talk about their bowels to others. She says we're getting a new cafeteria monitor next week.

The oldsters do love their intestinal chats

I never wished for Miss B. to get sick. At least, I never actually threw more than three bucks in quarters into a fountain when I wished I for it. But if she had to get sick, it really is sort of like an **Act of Justice** that it was the meat loaf that did her in.

It almost makes me believe that, in addition to fairies like the Tooth Fairy, there's a Fairy of Food Poisoning.

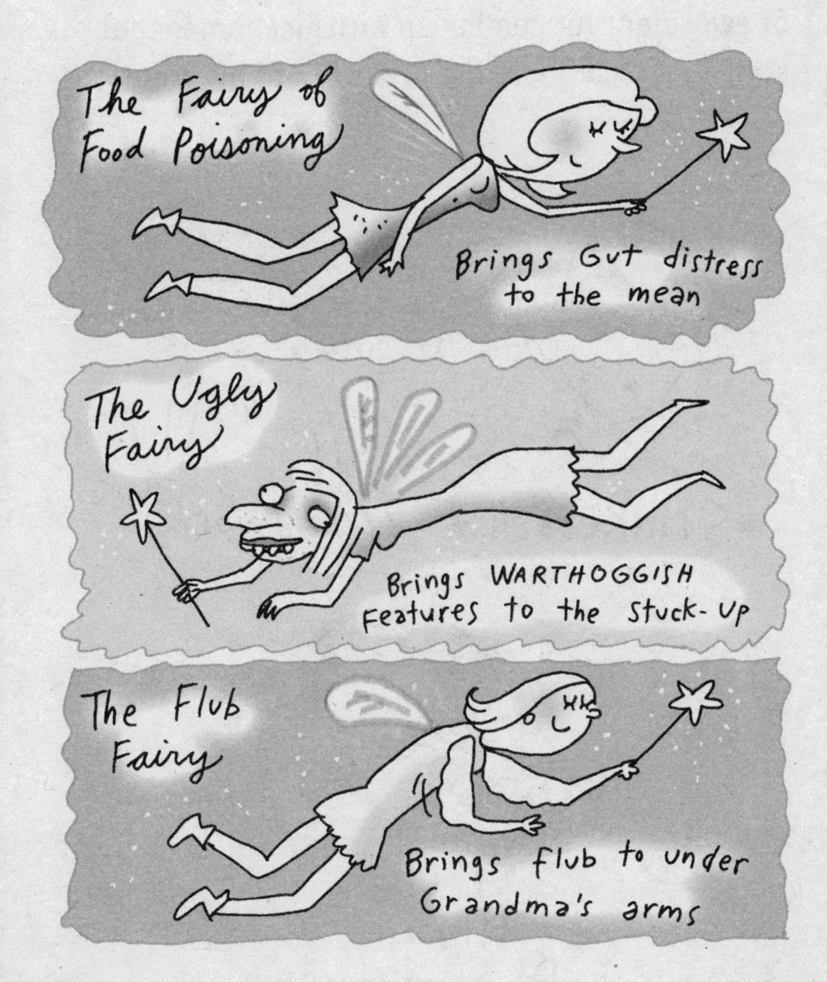

The Fairy of Food Poisoning
Brings Gut distress to the mean
The Ugly Fairy
Brings WARTHOGGISH Features to the Stuck-up
The Flub Fairy
Brings flub to under Grandma's arms

Mike Pinsetti gurgled up to the table while Isabella and I were eating.

Mike Pinsetti, you might remember, is the official nicknamer of the school. He has some sort of evil talent for coming up with nicknames that sting and stick. Here are just a few of his creations:

Anyway, I made the mistake of accidentally smiling at him once, and I'm afraid that now he is under the delusion that I think of him as, you know . . .

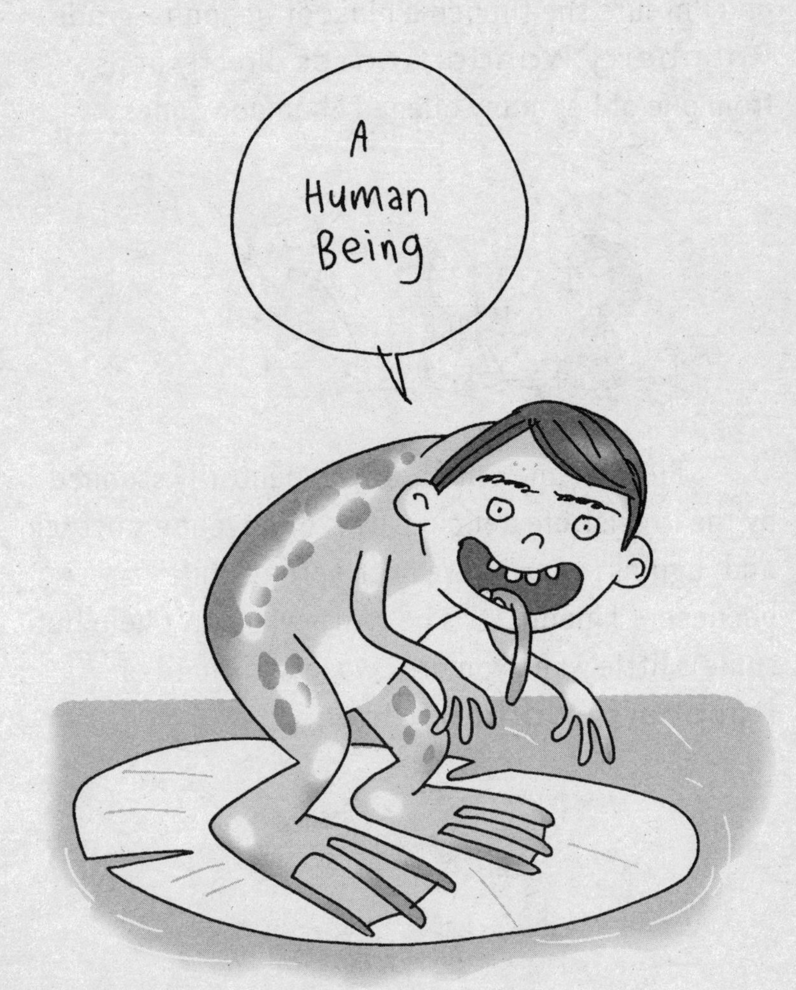

So Pinsetti is standing there with Isabella, and I'm just staring at him and I think he's trying to say something to me. But just as I went to perform **Dirty Look Number Four,** Angeline walks past and I'm sure she flipped a blast of weapons-grade **Raspberry Wonderfulness** directly at us from one of her many alleged Shampoo Zones.

Pinsetti and I are both momentarily stunned by the irresistible deliciousness of Angeline's attack and, against our will, we both sort of smile because — I mean, let's be real — you can't help but smile a little when you are awash in a cloud of **Raspberry Wonderfulness.**

So then, thanks to Angeline, Pinsetti and I are looking into each other's eyes while the bottom halves of our faces are smiling, and we are — I'm going to be sick — ***sharing*** this moment. And at the same time we're both trapped inside — I'm going to be even sicker — a fog of Angeline's stink.

Isabella said she could practically see **Pure Love** squirting out of Pinsetti's ears. I said it was for Angeline, but Isabella said it was for me. So don't be alarmed, Dumb Diary, if I wake up screaming several times throughout the night.

Saturday 07

Dear Dumb Diary,

Saturdays are so cool that I will never ever figure out why they only made one of them per week. Here's my idea for a whole new lineup of days:

SATURDAY
I can't improve on Saturday so I'm not changing it.

SUNTURDAY
This will be another Saturday, but it will also have the aimless Quality of a Sunday.

MONTURDAY
You can't get all your fun into just two Saturdays, so this is a bonus third.

WEEKSDAY
NOBODY LIKES WEEKDAYS. (THAT'S WHY THEY'RE CALLED "WEAK DAYS") LET'S GET THEM ALL OVER IN A SINGLE DAY.

FRIDAY
OK, IT'S A WEEKDAY BUT FRIDAYS ARE VERY IMPORTANT for PLANNING YOUR SATURDAYS.

FRIDAYNIGHTDAY
THIS IS AN ENTIRE DAY THAT'S NOTHING BUT FRIDAY NIGHT, ALL DAY LONG.

I called Isabella to see if she wanted to do something today, but her mom said she was at the mall with her dad. **I could hardly believe it!** Isabella has identified the five most embarrassing things a dad can do in public, and her dad does four of them:

DANCES
permits self to be witnessed in bathing suit
DResses like Lady for Halloween
Talks

For the rest of the day, I was grabbing the phone every time it rang, figuring it was Isabella calling me back. Late in the afternoon, some woman who sounded familiar called for Mom, but I couldn't quite place the voice. Afterward, Mom was all excited but wouldn't tell me who it was or why she called. Some dumb Mom-thing, I'm sure, like they're going shopping for wind chimes or something.

Other Dumb Things Moms Have
Need for birdbaths
Delight over tiny decorative soaps you're not allowed to actually use
Infantile joy when using puppetish oven mitts

Sunday 08

Dear Dumb Diary,

Saturdays rule! But I really don't mind Sundays, either. They're sort of like Saturday's less popular and less attractive little sister. She tries to be as fun as her older sister, but she still has to keep reminding you that you have homework due tomorrow and you have nothing to wear and there's a good chance Dad will be hogging the TV all day.

if days were people...

Saturday Sunday Wednesday

When I went downstairs for breakfast this morning, Mom was bustling around the kitchen all giddy and dazed, and said I could have candy for breakfast if I would just go eat it in front of the TV.

For as long as I can remember, Mom has practiced this sort of Motherly Irresponsibility whenever she wanted me out of the way. One time, I walked in on her when she was trying to force her mombutt into an old miniskirt and she was so embarrassed, she told me I could go outside and throw apples at passing cars if I'd leave her alone.

I knew her judgment was way off on that one so I didn't take her up on it, but candy for breakfast seemed only mildly self-destructive. I accepted her terms and let her have her ridiculous secret kitchen time.

Later on, Mom was cooking up a storm. Like most storms, we anticipated great devastation in its wake. You'll recall that Mom has cooked up a few memorable storms in the past. . . .

Like the Lasagna Dad and I felt was made with ferret.

But here's the weird thing: She cooked it, but she never actually inflicted it upon us. We smelled her cooking, we heard her cooking. Stinker even took the customary precaution of hiding his dog dish. But for some reason, Mom just packed it all up in a Tupperware container, stuck it in the fridge, and ordered a pizza.

Believe me: Dad and I did not ask questions. That would be like reminding your executioner not to forget his ax tomorrow.

Monday 09

Dear Dumb Diary,

Today in English class, Mr. Evans started our unit on fairy tales. We're discussing a few old favorites in class in order to understand what he expects from us on our reports. He started with *Hansel and Gretel,* which is about this witch who wants to eat a couple of grimy brats even though her entire house is made out of candy. I said that she was probably trying to drop a few pounds: **Children are high protein, low carb.**

Then we discussed *Snow White,* and *Rapunzel* and *Little Red Riding Hood,* and when Mr. Evans asked us what we thought of these fairy tales, I said that it was coming through loud and clear that back in olden times, if you had a really weird dumb name, you were probably just waiting for something disastrous to happen to you. I mean, you never hear about *Jennifer and the Seven Dwarves* or *Steve and the Three Bears*. Mr. Evans probably agreed with me deep down, but he bulged his Big Ol' Ugly Head Vein at me a little, anyway.

Jennifer and the Seven Dwarves

Lunchtime, Dumb Diary, was really something interesting today. It was even more interesting than when the lunch ladies had that dispute that started with angry words over who looked better in their hairnet, and ended with paramedics siphoning cranberry sauce out of a semi-plugged lunch-lady esophagus. (Note: In these sorts of situations, always bet on the more massive lunch lady.)

As I said, the school has somebody filling in for Miss Bruntford while her organs are healing or whatever. His name is Mr. Prince ("Prince!" Couldn't you just die?) He's a student teacher, which is a person who will become a teacher unless something better occurs to them at the last minute.

He is older without being fully old yet, which means he probably shaves more than twice a week but still does not have hairy ears.

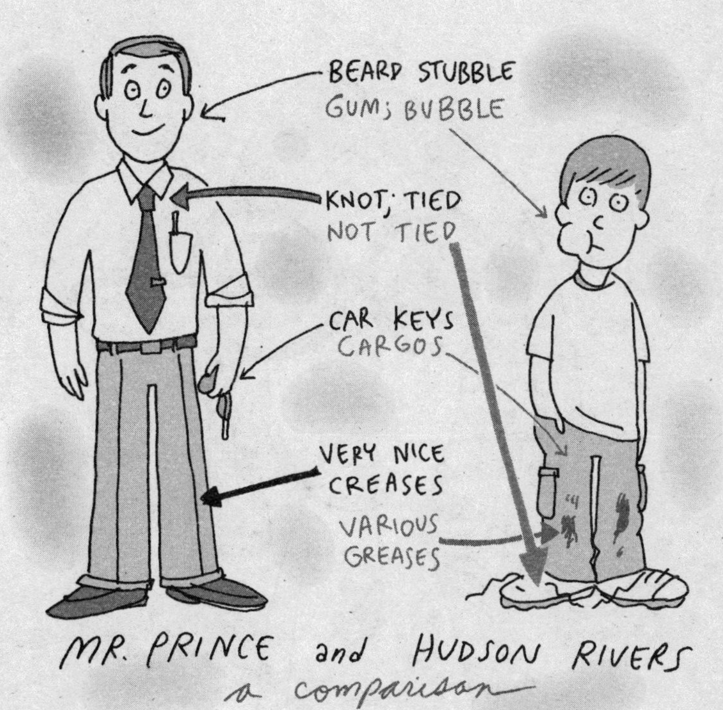

Furthermore, Angeline walked right past Mr. Prince (Possibly firing Zone after scented Zone at him? It remains a theory.) and he did not even look at her, which I think is evidence that he is not into that whole gorgeous-with-excellently-perfect-blond-hair thing. But who can blame him? Nobody really cares.

Isabella said he is probably into dark-haired girls with round glasses, and I had to remind her that I don't wear glasses.

But Isabella was impolitely hinting that Mr. Prince would like her better than me, which is pretty rude since I had already started thinking he would like me better than her, and I felt like I had to tell her so and also execute a mild version of **Dirty Look Number Three.** Plus, I may have pointed out how her head is almost a perfect sphere, and she is **NOT** at all secure about her cranial roundness.

This turned out to be a pretty bad idea since — and I have shared this with you before, Dumb Diary — Isabella has older brothers, which means she is very good at all forms of fighting.

Isabella stood up in the middle of the cafeteria, smiled at me and said, with perfect sinister cruelty: "Let's see how he likes you when he sees your picture hanging up in the cafeteria side-by-side with your dumpy little beagle."

When I got home, I took a good hard look at Stinker. He's too old and fat to run any more, and he does not hesitate to express a sudden and extreme interest in his own body parts even when he knows you're right there in the room having a conversation with him. I can't stand the idea of being compared to him.

I'm going to have to sweet-talk Isabella out of this project.

My Dog, Stinker

Tuesday 10

Dear Dumb Diary,

Okay, you can't sweet-talk Isabella out of anything. I explained to her today that I'm going to be totally embarrassed and humiliated when her project gets hung up, and instead of understanding and agreeing to scrap the whole idea like a best friend should, Isabella pretended to cry and said I was criticizing her art project.

When somebody actually pretends to cry as good as Isabella can pretend, and they really very nearly appear sad, you just have to back off.

In my defense, Isabella's pretend crying is better than most people's real crying, a skill she likely perfected to get her older brothers in trouble.

I thought about asking Isabella over for dinner, to take another crack at changing her mind, but Isabella, like all of my friends, sort of doesn't know how to interpret a dinner invitation. Everybody is aware of my mom's cooking challenges, even the teachers.

It's like if you were Dracula's kid and you asked somebody over for a neck massage.

None of this really matters much, because I had a long conversation over lunch today with Mr. Prince. (Couldn't You Just Die?)

It happened as I was taking my tray to the trash. I had done a particularly thorough job of abusing my leftover food today. I had shoved the macaroni and cheese into a large wad, stuck a carrot stick straight up in it, and dumped chocolate milk over the whole thing.

Mr. Prince (C.Y.J.D.?) was standing by the trash, and when I went to slide it in, he looked at it and said, "That a model of the Eiffel Tower?" and kind of laughed a little.

"*Sí,*" I said, not wanting to miss out on his reference to All Things French. And then I threw my garbage in the can and ran away.

Okay, Dumb Diary, I know. I know. Strictly speaking, "*sí*" is not exactly French for "yes." It's Spanish. But Spain and France are sort of the same big CountryOverThere and I was a bit flustered that he wanted to have a long conversation with me. Besides, I'm confident he knows that, even though I didn't actually speak French, I implied French.

It was a moment, Dumb Diary. We shared a moment.

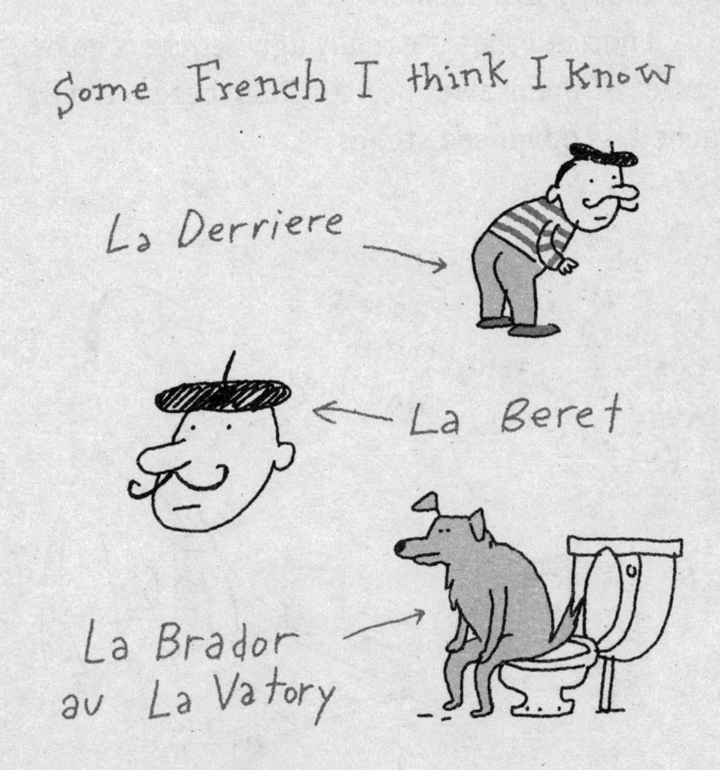

Wednesday 11

Dear Dumb Diary,

Art class today. Angeline has collected almost half of the teacher's childhood pictures already. I did my part of the project by pasting them to the poster board and writing the teacher's name underneath each one.

I noticed that the really ugly teachers gave pictures of themselves as little kids, before the Ugly reached its advanced stages.

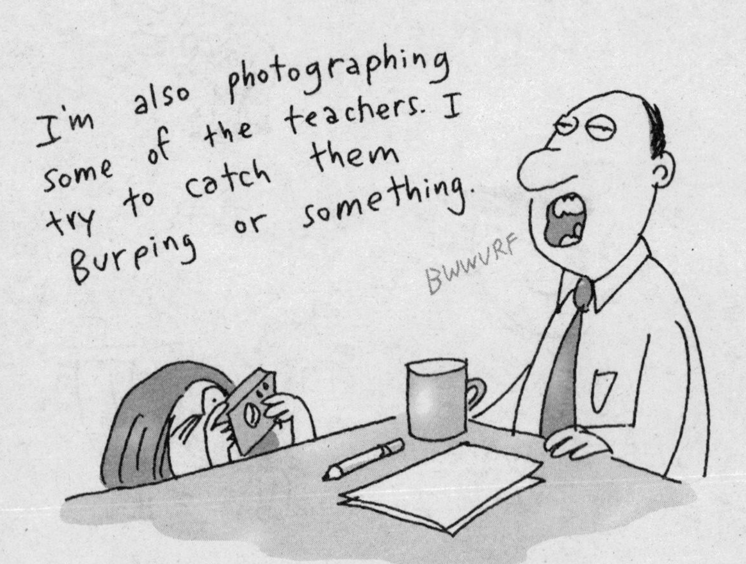

I'm also photographing some of the teachers. I try to catch them Burping or something.
BWWVRF

Miss Anderson's picture just happens to be from when she was about seventeen and a half. She just happened to be at the beach and she just happened to be in an adorable pose. I have seen so many pictures of these adorable poses that I'm starting to think that really pretty girls stay in these poses all the time, just in case somebody whips out a camera.

Miss Anderson reminded us that we all had to get in our pictures for Isabella's project and that if somebody doesn't have a pet, they could just give Isabella a picture of an animal they resemble.

Of course, I saw my opportunity here, and after dinner I encouraged Stinker to run away from home. I might have gotten away with it except that the neighbors across the street called my parents to report that I had left the front door open and that I had thrown about twelve dollars worth of pork chops across the street onto their lawn.

Seriously. "Why ***wouldn't*** a fat ugly beagle chase after twelve dollars worth of pork chops?" I screamed as I picked up the raw chops and put them in a trash bag, out in the rain, alone in the dark. The neighbors watched me from behind their curtains like the timid, tattletaling turds they are.

Anyway, now that I think about it, even if Stinker had run away from home, he might only be gone three or four days. He's done it before, and that's usually how long it takes before he decides to come back.

Thursday 12

Dear Dumb Diary,

Mr. Evans had to remind us again today that our fairy-tale report is due in a couple of weeks. Then we read a few more fairy tales and talked about them.

We started with *The Princess and the Pea,* which is probably the most exciting and thrilling story ever written about somebody having mild insomnia. I said that it teaches us that you probably don't want to sleep in a bed that somebody has pead.

This **sounds** a lot different than it looks when you write it, but I think Mr. Evans cut me some slack because now he thinks I have seizures.

Hey, Dumb D, here's something new: This was the first Thursday since I've been at Mackerel Middle School when we were not forcibly meatloafed. We were all sort of mystified, but nobody was complaining.

And here is something else new (although it really shouldn't be). When I went to my locker today, somebody had romantically slid a note in through the odor vents.

I can hardly believe it! Here it is:

THE LOVE THAT CANNOT BE

A moment shared, a smile bright
As any smile can be,
So sad, yet so enchanting,
The Love that cannot be.

Signed,
M.P.

CAN YOU BELIEVE IT? "M. P." It's from Mr. Prince! I would love to smash this note in Angeline's face and also smash it slightly lighter in Isabella's. It's ME that he noticed. Not Blondie, Not Sphere-Head. ME! And even though he knows that we can never be together — because I am normal-aged and he is old — he still needed to give his heart voice. How he must suffer and ache. I wonder if he yearned for me. This could be the first time I had caused a yearn. (Or is that a "yearning"? "yearnfulness"? "yearnation"?)

I showed the poem to Isabella and I think she may be a little jealous. I wonder if Mr. Prince would wait for me to grow up?

While waiting for you to grow up, a person should be allowed to read or listen quietly to the radio

Friday 13

Dear Dumb Diary,

I forgave Isabella again. It's amazing how just knowing that Mr. Prince wrote me a love poem makes me feel so confident. Isabella's meanness to me kind of dissolved away like blueberry stains on a denture commercial. (Note to old people: There are many other less inky pies to enjoy.)

Also, Isabella has very strong powers of persuasion.

Maybe somebody should invent toothpaste pie for denture wearers

I asked Isabella if she wanted to go to the mall with me this weekend, but she said she was going with her dad again. I quizzed her on this — complete with gagging noises — and she refused to talk about it. Isabella is up to something, Dumb Diary. I can tell.

Some of Isabella's Schemes
Tried to fly with Balloons. (first grade)
Attempted to acheive tan with flashlights. (wasted over 40 batteries)

Masqueraded as weathergirl to try to get principal to declare snow day in May.

I made another little garbage sculpture for Mr. Prince today. This one was a wadded-up lump of cheeseburger with some fries stuck in it to resemble the Statue of Liberty's head (in keeping with our cute French thing). Before I slid it into the trash can, I tried to direct Mr. Prince's attention to it with head nods and eyebrow twitches until I saw Mr. Evans coming at me with that **You're-Having-Another-Seizure** look in his eyes and I had to dump and run.

Mr. Prince and I are practically like Cinderella and Prince Charming except that, in our case, Cinderella is mutilating her food for attention and exhibits false seizure symptoms, and Prince Charming isn't all obsessed with footwear. But other than that . . .

Seriously, wouldn't it have been easier for the prince to just recognize Cinderella's FACE?

I gave some more thought to helping Stinker run away from home this afternoon. After school, I made him watch a show on wolves on The Discovery Channel, hoping that maybe it would make him want to run wild and perhaps haul his chubby rump up some mountain and howl at the moon. But I don't think he understood.

Not even when I got a big round pillow and tried to make him howl at it by holding it over his face. I was only playing, but Stinker seemed to get a little panicky, and his wolf howl sounded a little like a whine.

He was so upset afterward that it took him, like, thirty minutes of constant gnawing on his chew toy (which I have named **Grossnasty**) to calm down.

I have no idea how I'm going to avoid giving Isabella a photo of Stinker.

Stinker goes freaky on Grossnasty

Late-Breaking News: Carryout tacos for dinner. Get this: Mom didn't have time to make dinner because she went to Miss Bruntford's house for a visit. MISS BRUNTFORD'S HOUSE!

Surprised, Dumb Diary? Me, too. I mean: **A house??** I always assumed Miss Bruntford lived under a bridge, where she asked travelers riddles before she'd let them pass.

Since when would Mom visit Miss Bruntford?

Who cares. Dad and I don't want to ask too many questions. I ate so many tacos, my neck hurts. Note to Taco Company: Invent a taco that one may consume without suffering head dislocation.

Seriously, can you imagine trying to invent a brand-new food nowadays and telling people that there's one catch: You have to be sideways to eat it?

People are willing to endure SIDEWAYS-HEAD-EATING FOR tacos, but would they do it for
a sideways cheeseburger?
or
Sideways spaghetti?

TACOS REMAIN YOUR BEST BET FOR SIDEWAYS-HEAD-EATING.

Saturday 14

Dear Dumb Diary,

It's amazing. On school days, when I get up early, I'm so exhausted I can hardly walk, but when I get up early on a Saturday, I'm not even tired. How do your muscles know what day it is?

I walked over to Isabella's this morning. I figured that if I just **happened** to be there when she and her dad went to the mall, they'd have to take me along.

When I got to Isabella's house, unbelievably, right in the middle of her front lawn was this incredibly cute puffball of a kitten. I scooped it up and knocked on her door. When Isabella answered, I thought her eyes were going to pop out of her head.

"Where'd you get that cat?" she said, in one of those whispers where you're kind of yelling and whispering at the same time. I told her I found it on her lawn. She said that it belonged to one of the neighbors and they were looking for it and I had to give it to her to return to them. That was all fine with me, but I couldn't help noticing that Isabella was breathing just like Stinker did when I had him under the pillow during his wolf training.

Then she took the kitten and said the mall trip was cancelled, she'd call me later, and then *SLAM.* Just that fast, I had been de-kittened, de-malled, and blown off by my best friend.

When I was walking home, thinking about things I'd like to happen to Isabella, and trying to look sad (I'm rather pretty when I'm sad), I had that feeling you get when you're being watched. I looked up, and there, in a minivan — which was not the giant golden carriage drawn by the perfect white horses you might expect — was Angeline. And when we locked eyes, she waved. Not a big You're-My-Best-Friend wave, but not one of those weird upright rotations that the girls on parade floats do, either.

This in itself was odd, as Angeline and I are not friends because she is too beautiful and stuck-up to be a friend, but what was ***really*** odd was her mom . . .

Angeline's wave appeared
almost human

I think this was the first time I had ever seen Angeline's mom, and I don't know what I would have expected, but it was not at all what I saw.

You know when a movie star brings one of her parents to an awards ceremony and you always think: Wow. Her parents are as ugly as mine. How did **THAT** happen?

That's kind of what it was like with Angeline's mom. Except not in the face.

Years ago, my folks and I were at the zoo, and a three-year-old, thinking he was looking at a porcupine or a sloth or something, tried to feed a peanut to the back of my head. It was at that moment that I knew I had **The World's Worst Hair.** That is, until now.

Angeline's mom had Angeline's beautiful face, but growing out in curly shiny sprouts here, and straight dry wisps there, her hair looked as though the stylist had misplaced her scissors and just tried chewing it off.

A handful of clips and ties and barrettes did nothing to improve things. It only made it look like she had stumbled into the display rack on her way out of the salon.

I believe that, somehow, while she was pregnant, the tiny, evil, infant Angeline spawn had totally sucked all the quality out of her mother's hair. I mean, what else could it be? Unless . . .

Unless this means that Angeline is going to grow up that way! Of course! Angeline is using up all of her **hairpretty** too soon. She's going to burn out.

As Angeline and her mom pulled away in their white minivan, I just stood there for a moment, confused and stunned . . . and happy. All I could think was that maybe, just like in fairy tales, **Dreams Really Do Come True.** Maybe there **IS** an Ugly Fairy, and one day, she will visit Angeline!

UGLY is so BEAUTIFUL when it happens to someone who Deserves it.

Sunday 15

Dear Dumb Diary,

It's Sunday and I figured I should start thinking about my fairy-tale report.

I've ruled out *The Pied Piper* since I don't buy kids following a flute player. A guitar, maybe, but not a flute.

I've also ruled out *The Emperor's New Clothes* because, well, simply put: **Ick.**

AND THUMBELINA IS KIND OF Scary to me...

So I've decided to do my report on *The Frog Prince.* The story really speaks to me, because I'm practically identical to the Princess in the story except that I don't have a frog to kiss and make into a Prince, but I do have a Prince (Mr. Prince) who loves a place where they eat frogs (France). **Gross.**

Okay, okay. Strictly speaking, not everybody in France eats frogs. And they only eat the legs, anyway. And lots of gross people everywhere eat frog legs, not just gross French people. Leave me alone. It's a good comparison.

I'm sure that Angeline is doing her report on *Rapunzel.* I mean, how could she **NOT** do it on *Rapunzel*? Here are a few versions of Rapunzel I'd like to see Angeline star in:

The Prince is allergic to Rapunzel's shampoo and has to climb up her eyelashes instead.

Prince is so fat that he pulls off Rapunzel's head.

Prince falls for a princess with brown hair of reasonable length. Rapunzel starves.

Monday 16

Dear Dumb Diary,

Another poem today from You-know-who!

THE FAIREST BLOSSOM

She is the fairest blossom. True,
She blooms in any weather.
But I must love her from afar.
We'll never be together.

Signed,
M.P.

Can you believe the pain he's in? His suffering? The crushing heartache he endures every time he sees me?

God, it just makes me so happy!

Also, it's like a totally amazing coincidence that he wrote about me as a blossom after I did the same thing in my poem to my mom. It's like we share a common head. Isn't that sweet?

ok, a little creepy maybe

I showed this one to Isabella, and I think she may be even a little jealouser. Yeah, I'm pretty sure he'll wait for me to grow up.

Tuesday 17

Dear Dumb Diary,

Today Mr. Evans told us that fairy tales were sometimes used to teach a lesson. He asked for examples and I said *Rumplestiltskin* taught an important lesson. (*Rumplestiltskin,* Dumb Diary, is the one about the creepy little guy who helps the imprisoned maiden spin gold from straw so she can escape a lifetime in jail, in exchange for her first-born baby.)

I said it taught us that pretty young maidens break deals all the time, even if you give them a mountain of gold and get them out of jail. If anything, I said, these pretty young maidens are the cause of all the trouble in the world, breaking into bears' houses and busting up their junk, antagonizing wolves, getting lost in the woods, making their stepmothers crazy. It goes on and on.

Mr. Evans's vein throbbed, and he said I was the first student that he had ever heard of rooting **for** *Rumplestiltskin* and **against** *Red Riding Hood,* which I thought might mean I was a genius.

But failing to cheer for the Goldilocks type is evidently a symptom of seizurism in Mr. Evans's book. So he sent me down to the nurse's office **AGAIN** for a little cot time. It's not a big deal anymore. The office ladies know me now and they just wave me in and I make myself comfortable. They even gave me my own key to the cot room this time and said that if I want different drapes in there or something, I can decorate it any way I want since I am the only one using it. This made them laugh at me a little, which made me say something like "old bats" or "old hags" or something like that. Anyway, I had to give the key back, and probably the drapes are out.

Wednesday 18

Dear Dumb Diary,

I found another poem in my locker this morning! ! ! ! ! ! ! ! ! ! ! ! ! ! ! ! ! !
! !
! !
! ! !

HEY, JAMIE, YOU ARE A CUTE GIRL,
NOT THE TYPE THAT WOULD MAKE ME HURL.
YOU'RE NOT AN OYSTER, YOU'RE A PEARL,
YOU'RE CUTEST IN THE WHOLE WIDE WORL.

SIGNED,
SECRET ADMIRER

Okay. So maybe it's not his best work. Even Shakespeare probably had some off days.

But let's not forget the yearning. It probably hurts when he yearns, and that's probably throwing off his poetry. Shut up. He's calling himself an *admirer* now.

I wonder if there's a store where you can buy pedestals for your admirer to worship you on.

I returned his sentiments with a token of my affection that I presented in the form of artistically fingered food at lunch. I had captured The Sphinx quite well, considering how infrequently The Ancient Egyptians sculpted in spaghetti and Jell-O. Even Isabella agreed, and she says that since she is Italian, she is an expert on pasta.

There was also a pyramid
but I ate it.

As I slid my love tribute into the garbage with a sad, slippery smush, Mr. Prince said that I had done a fabulous job and that, even covered in spaghetti sauce, my hands still looked like beautiful petite little doves that were bleeding badly (and at which somebody had thrown Jell-O).

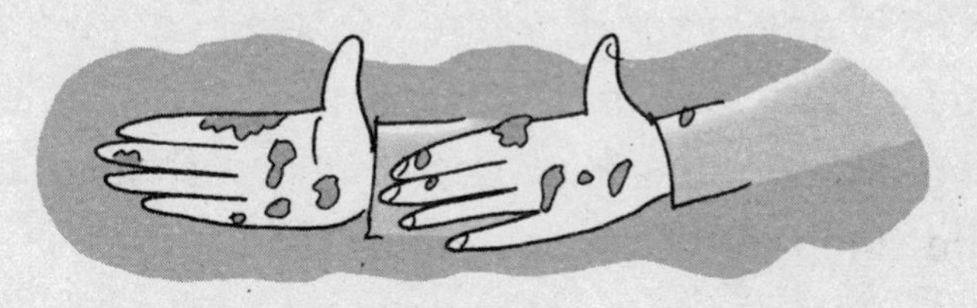

He didn't exactly say that **mouthfully**. He said it more with his eyes. Or maybe I read his mind. I don't know. Anyway, when I turned around, Hudson was right behind me in line and he said "Hi," but since I'm sort of involved with Mr. Prince right now, I had taken a few steps before I even realized that Hudson had been speaking to me, so I didn't respond.

Angeline was right there, too, and she seemed a bit surprised. Maybe she was surprised by Mr. Prince's yearning. Or maybe she was surprised that I had blown off Hudson. Or maybe she was surprised to learn that The Sphinx would have looked better with a big meatball nose.

In any event, I'm sure I noticed her give her head a little forward flip, casting her hair fumes at poor unsuspecting Hudson, who I now think of as a child compared to my charming Mr. Prince.

Angeline looking confused.
Look how She even has to have pretty question marks in her head.

Thursday 19

Dear Dumb Diary,

First thing this morning, I took another shot at Isabella. I tried to get her to let me say that I didn't have a pet, but she said that would undermine her integrity as an artist. I reminded her that last month she turned in a drawing she had done of Angelina Jolie for her self-portrait assignment.

I asked her if I could just use a picture of a different beagle, like, one that was less of a disgusting slobber-mouthed odor museum than Stinker, but she said that would be dishonest. Then I reminded her that two months ago, she had drawn on her glasses with a marker in order to make everybody think she had blue eyes.

I asked her if she really believed that people look like their pets, and she said that it was not her but Science that had made this decision. I then reminded her that judging by the shape of her head, she must have a balloon for a pet.

Which meant, of course, that we did not eat lunch together today.

At least there was no meat loaf for the second Thursday in a row, and no Miss Bruntford, either. I wonder if they've just decided to keep Mr. Prince on permanently. That would be excellently awesome, of course, although I suppose I should consider Mr. Prince's pain.

Okay, I considered it. It would still be excellently awesome.

While you wait for me to grow up...

You may not DATE.
In fact, just stay indoors.

Try to stay up on fashion trends so when I show up you're not all 20-YEARS-AGO.

Spend time each day thinking about hair that is not blond. Or red. Or black. Or nice.

Friday 20

Dear Dumb Diary,

Angeline stopped by my locker this morning, and she had "our" art project almost completely finished, except that she wanted me to apply the glitter. No surprise, really. I'm known widely for my skills with glue and glitter, or **Glittifying,** as those of us in the biz like to call it.

Angeline had pictures of all the teachers when they were younger. Some were babies, some were teens. I have to admit, for a minute, it seemed like this **WAS** a pretty good idea.

But then I saw the picture labeled "Bruntford."

It looked like a kindergarten photo of a plain-looking little girl . . . who looked like me. And not just a little bit like me, Dumb Diary. She looked totally exactly **precisely** like me.

You know what this means? It means that if Miss Bruntford looked like **ME** when she was a kid, then I'm going to look like **HER** when I'm an adult!

"Does it look okay?" Angeline said, all smuglike. "I hope you don't mind that I did the glitter myself. I'm going to drop it off with Miss Anderson now, so she can put it up in the cafeteria next week."

And then Angeline paused for just a second, with this strange kind of tiny smile that was as small and bewildering as a baby's butt.

I know that she noticed the resemblance in Miss Bruntford's photo and she wanted me to crumble.

But I didn't. I stayed strong and silent and just nodded okay, thinking that this was even worse than Isabella's project, and wondering why I had thought there was something bewildering about baby butts.

Next week, both Isabella's *and* Angeline's projects go up in the cafeteria, and everybody — including Mr. Prince — will see them.

I very much doubt that even *Rumplestiltskin* can save me now.

But maybe Humpty Dumpty could

Saturday 21

Dear Dumb Diary,

When I woke up this morning, I knew this might be my last chance to persuade Isabella to change her project. I hoped that when I told her about Baby Bruntford, she might take pity on me and change her mind. I was also fully prepared to lie and say her head was becoming less round. (When in reality, if anything, it's getting rounder.)

How Isabella should Bowl

When I got to Isabella's house, there on her front lawn was the kitten I found last week, along with another one. I scooped them up and rang the doorbell. Isabella was holding a third, much younger kitten in her arms when she opened the door. When she saw me standing there with the other two kittens, she looked just like she did after we learned about **you-know-what** in biology.

"Oh, good," she lied.

Isabella can lie to almost anybody but me. I can always spot her deceptions, and she usually doesn't bother even trying. The fact that she was even trying indicated that she was really and truly desperate.

"My neighbors lost those two kittens that you have there, as well as this third kitten, which I found just before you got here. Let me have them all and I'll return them promptly to their rightful owners, which is not me. And hurry up, because my mom is here and I don't want her to see them, because (Isabella was really groping for an explanation here) because . . . my . . . mom . . . has . . . a . . . real . . . soft . . . spot . . . for . . . baby . . . animals."

Isabella's mom is really nice and everything, but a soft spot for baby animals? I've seen her pound veal like it owed her money.

Sunday 22

Dear Dumb Diary,

I launched Operation Beagle Bounce today and it failed. I blame coffee and dog breeding.

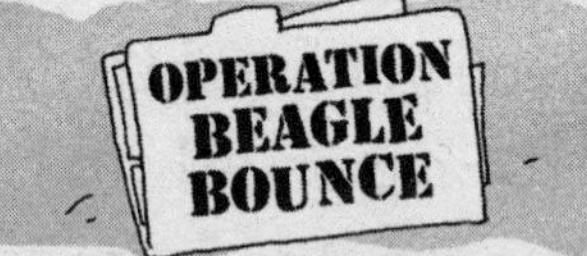

The idea came to me last night, as I watched Stinker gnaw/make-out with Grossnasty, his chew toy.

I really thought this plan could not miss, and here's how it came together:

While my parents were asleep, I put a couple of aspirin bottles and a Kleenex box on Mom's bedside table. I dumped all the coffee beans in the trash and left the empty bag on the counter. Then I changed Dad's alarm clock.

I got dressed for school and picked up my backpack and tiptoed into my parent's room. Then I shook my dad and said, "Dad. Dad. Look at the time! You're late! You're late!" I had to sound really freaked out or it might occur to him that today was Sunday and he didn't have to go to work at all.

The first thing he did was look at my mom, who was still asleep. I pointed at the aspirin and Kleenex. "Don't wake Mom. I don't think she feels well."

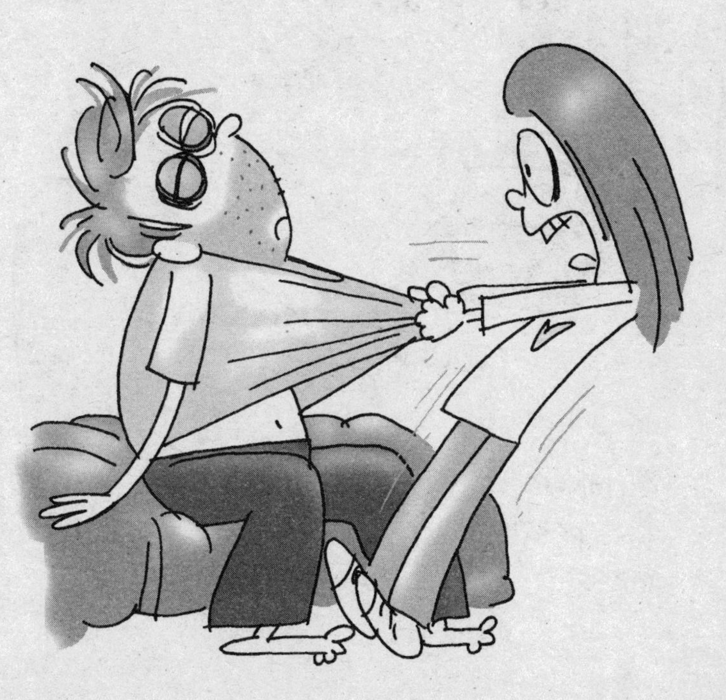

Dad jumped into his clothes and came downstairs. I couldn't have him hanging around to maybe wake up Mom. I pointed at the coffeepot: "Out of coffee: Dad, go go go!" Dad ran to his car and hopped in, not noticing that I was right behind him, carrying fat ol' Stinker out to the driveway. He also failed to notice that somebody had tied Grossnasty to the back bumper of his car.

Dad already drives too fast, but when he thinks he's late for work, he shoots out of the driveway like a rocket. I figured that when Stinker saw Grossnasty taking off, he'd trot behind the car for a while, fussing and wheezing until he eventually got tired and lost. Then somebody would pick him up and return him to us. I figured he'd be back by the end of the week, and by that time, I would have been allowed to submit a picture of a beautiful fawn or swan or something to Isabella's project, because I did not have a pet anymore — my pet had run away.

Oooooh
maybe
a swan
that
can do
BALLET!

But here's how dog breeding works, I guess. Long ago, people who wanted to invent the beagle looked around for the beagliest animals they could find. And when those two beaglish dogs had puppies, they married those puppies to other super-beagly dogs, until finally, after they did this a jillion times, they got the beagle as we know it today.

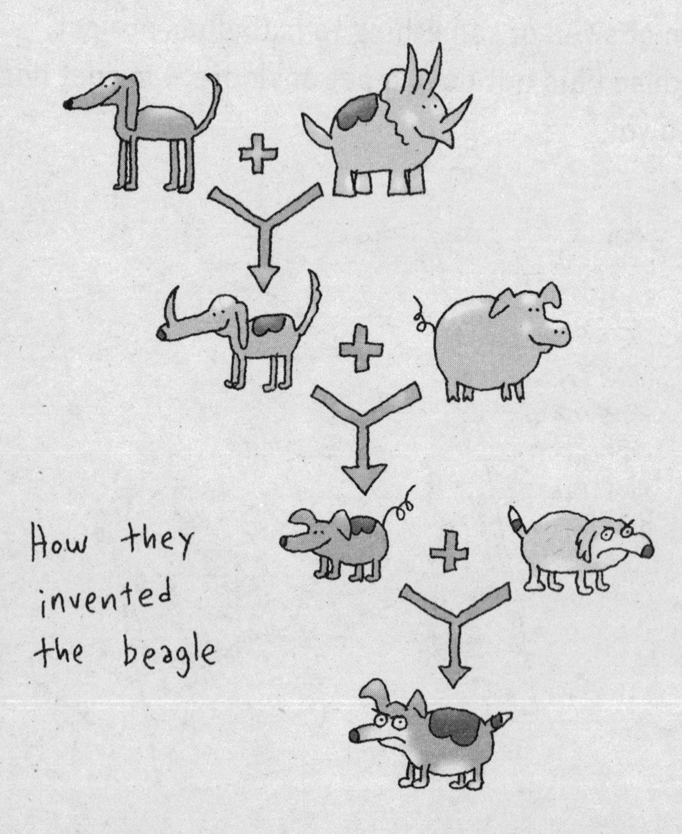
How they invented the beagle

I had never really thought about what beagles had been bred *for*. I suppose I thought they were bred to stink and be nuisances, like maybe for homeowners who wanted something to dig up their flower beds but were afraid the neighbors would object to a skunk.

But it turns out, beagles were bred to chase things, fast things, like foxes and — at this particular moment — chew toys tethered to moving cars.

Stinker took off faster than I had ever seen him move. I could barely hear Dad's tires squealing over the sound of Stinker's toenails scraping on the cement. Stinker caught up to Dad's car quickly and got a good chomp on Grossnasty.

And I learned that there's another thing that beagles were bred to do: **Not Give Up.** Stinker was not going to let go of Grossnasty for anything, not even to avoid being dragged behind a car.

Fortunately (for Stinker), Dad only went a block or so before he had to stop.

For medicine? For gasoline? Nope.

For coffee. Adults' bloodstreams are practically full of it, and my dad is maybe the worst. Since he didn't get it at home, he was willing to be late for work just for a cup of his precious Starbucks. ("Need some latte in my batte," he always says.)

When Dad got out of the car, he noticed Stinker still hanging on to Grossnasty and realized, by looking at a newspaper box outside Starbucks, that it was Sunday.

When Dad got home, he was pretty angry, but I apologized as hard as I could for getting the calendar mixed up, and he just grumped a little, handed me Stinker (who was scruffier and dirtier than ever), and went back to bed.

Like I said, the plan had failed, and it looked like I wasn't going to get rid of Stinker. But then, at that time, I hadn't considered **The Mom Factor.**

Mom sprang her big surprise on us this afternoon.

Remember last week when somebody called and Mom got all excited? It was Miss Bruntford. She had asked Mom for her meat loaf recipe so they could use it to make the **New Improved** school meat loaf.

All the teachers know about my Mom's cooking. Last year, the lemon squares my mom brought for a bake sale caused a dozen kids to lose their hearing for three days.

And one kid says that everything he eats still tastes lemony.

Mom says she made a little loaf (remember that day when we smelled her cooking but she gave us pizza?) and took it over to Miss Bruntford's. Miss B. tried it, and asked Mom to make a big batch to try on the kids this week at school.

Mom says that Miss Bruntford knows the kids hate the school meat loaf, and she thinks my mom can solve the problem. Mom is so proud of herself that Dad and I were careful not to say anything discouraging. Though I did overhear Dad make a secret call to our insurance agent to see if we were covered if Mom food-poisoned an entire middle school.

No, No. Not the Lemon Squares again. Meat Loaf.

So Mom spent the entire day making her meat loaves.

I was in the family room trying not to inhale any more meat loaf odor than I had to when I saw Stinker walk into the kitchen and then walk out. He scratched at the door to go outside. I opened it and he walked down the sidewalk and slowly down the street.

I watched him walk all the way out of sight.

When I looked in the kitchen, I saw what Stinker had seen. Not just a couple of meat loaves, but countless steaming football-shaped meat lumps stacked on every counter.

And I understood: Stinker had done the math. He knows how much leftover meat loaf he is expected to eat from one single meat loaf. The leftovers he thought he was going to have to eat from this batch were just too much to bear.

Mom said that one day I'd appreciate her cooking, and she was right: Today I do.

Stinker has run away from home!

The glorious stink
of it all!

Monday 23

Dear Dumb Diary,

That's right! Stinker has run away from home, and Isabella ***still*** won't let me off the hook. She says the law states that unless the dog is gone forever, or has been given away, or the dog or turtle has been replaced with a different kitten, then it's still my dog, and that's what is going in the project.

I asked her if she meant "puppy" instead of "kitten," and she got all panicky again and said it could be a puppy or a kitten and, besides, those weren't her kittens.

Then she added that I wouldn't need to give her my photos. She already had pictures of me and Stinker that were going to work just fine for her art project.

I wondered if today would be a good day to have a long talk with Mr. Prince, maybe sort out some of these feelings we have for each other, and see if he could get Isabella suspended.

I thought I'd hint at it a little by sculpting Isabella's head in mashed potatoes with a fork stuck in one eye.

He didn't notice, though. He wasn't standing by the garbage can today. Mr. Prince was off in a corner talking with Miss Anderson. Probably asking about me. He cares so much.

I think Hudson may have said hi to me today, but I didn't really notice, being so deeply immersed in the romantic fairy tale that is my life, although I still really can't tell if I'm the Princess or the frog. (This fairy-tale report for Evans is going to be tough.)

Also I was pretty hungry and wished that I had eaten Isabella's head instead of throwing it out.

Wait a second. Why did Isabella bring up those kittens again?

Tuesday 24

Dear Dumb Diary,

That was the very first thing I asked Isabella today. I also asked her if the neighbors got their kittens back and if the kittens were happy now and kittens **kittens KITTENS.**

And it was more than Isabella could take. She knows she can't lie to me. It was time for her to give up trying.

She said it had come to her in a flash in art class that nobody had an uglier pet than I do. Except her. Isabella has a turtle.

So she used her powers of persuasion on her dad to make him take her to the mall to get a kitten, which is one of the all-time cutest animals in the world.

But Isabella says that in as little as a week kitten cuteness starts to fade. And she wanted her pet to be ***the*** cutest one in the project so that everybody would say that Isabella was the cutest girl in our grade.

So she told her dad that the kitten had run away, and she cried and cried until he took her to get a new one. (As you might recall, Dumb Diary, Isabella's fake crying is unrivaled.)

The replacement kitten also started to lose its cuteness after a week, so she replaced it the same way. She's keeping the extras hidden in her room until the assignment is over.

See?
Kitten
cuteness
can
spoil.
Who Knew?

So I had her, right? In my best TV lawyer voice, I pointed out that the **TURTLE** is the real pet and **that's** what has to be in the photo.

Then she got all sinister again and smiled this real horrible smile. "Nope," she said. "Last night, kittens one and two ate the turtle. A shame, really, but it all works out fine in the end."

"But it doesn't work out fine for me. Not for ME!" I said.

And she countered with — get this —"What do you care, with your three boyfriends?"

"Three boyfriends?" I said. "WHAT three boyfriends?"

She never answered. She just said that she had even worse pictures of me and Stinker, and if I knew what was good for me, I'd just be quiet about the kittens until the assignment was over.

Isabella has older brothers and is therefore an expert in blackmail.

Other bad pictures Isabella probably has. I'm sure the ones of me are similar.

Wednesday 25

Dear Dumb Diary,

We turned in our art projects today. Isabella was glaring at me and flashed the more awful pictures of me and Stinker, just to keep me in line.

PICTURES TOO HORRIBLE
TO SHOW EVEN IN
MY OWN DIARY

Angeline kept looking at me like she expected me to say something to her, but what did I have to say? I'm either Miss Bruntford or The Beagle. I was done talking.

mine is a
nightmare.
How's
YOUR
Life?

And at lunch today, Pinsetti was jabbering so loud at me, I couldn't hear what Mr. Prince and Miss Anderson were saying, but they were giggling, so I suppose it was about something funny I had said.

The only good thing, I guess, is that Hudson and Angeline were sitting together. I'm grateful that she's taken him off my hands—although as I write this, I can hardly believe I said that. As a matter of fact, I take it back . . .

But I guess that just shows how committed I am to making Mr. Prince wait painfully for me until I am an adult.

Maybe he could carve me out of things while he waits...
me carved out of granite
me carved out of marble
me carved out of a larger sculpture of me

Thursday 26

Dear Dumb Diary,

Miss Bruntford and Mom's meat loaf are back!

We all knew this day would come. But what I didn't expect was my mom to show up as well. When your mom shows up at school unexpectedly, you figure that either your house burned down or she read your diary.

But my mom was just excited to see the kids enjoy her meat loaf. "I told you that you'd appreciate my cooking one day," she said.

The kids were sitting down with Mom's meat loaf just as Miss Anderson waltzed into the cafeteria and started hanging up the photo assignments. The embarrassment was going to be horrific. I started wondering what my first few therapists were going to be like.

But then a kid screamed as if something had stabbed the inside of his mouth.

It was the meat loaf!

Another kid ran out of the cafeteria covering his mouth, then another. Mom looked distressed, but Miss Bruntford looked absolutely delighted. Way too delighted.

Delighted as if she had planned it this way all along . . .

Then it all became clear to me. As the cafeteria emptied itself of sickened kids, I realized that Miss Bruntford's diabolical scheme was much like Isabella's plan to make herself look better BY COMPARISON.

Miss Bruntford's solution was to make the kids eat an **even worse** meat loaf recipe. That way, from that point on, the regular school meat loaf would seem less horrible BY COMPARISON.

The cafeteria was empty of kids now, except for me and Angeline — who had not yet taken a bite of her meat loaf. She walked right over to Isabella's project, tore off the picture of Stinker, and replaced it with a different photo she'd pulled out of her pocket.

It was a photo of a beautiful, stunning, immaculately groomed beagle like you'd see on the cover of *American Beagle* magazine.

"It's Stinker," she said.

"I found him wandering around near our garbage cans last night. He was pretty scruffy-looking, so I washed him up a little. Looked like he had been dragged, if you can believe it.

"I started out with a warm mineral water rinse, then a massage with a diluted baby shampoo. I used a protein-enriched aloe base on his face and head, slowly moving toward a hydrating sheen enhancer along his back. I hit his legs with an herbal, of course, and tipped his tail with a peroxide scrubbing to bring out the white. Then I used a multiplex conditioner with some modifications I made just for the complexities of a beagle's coat, and I trimmed him up, too, using my silver feathering-blade scissors that I bought on eBay. They only manufactured six of these, and five of them have never been outside Hollywood.

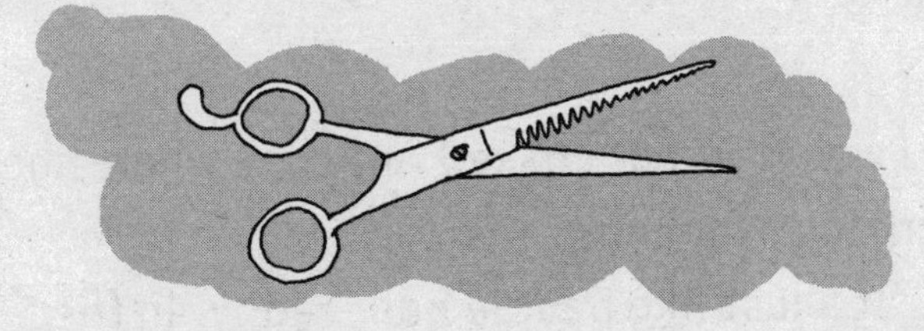

"I figured that this is how he should look in his photo. He's at my house right now. You can pick him up whenever you want."

She handed me the horrible shot of Stinker that she had pulled down. It was an **Extreme Makeover Moment.**

I was floored. I asked Angeline where she learned dog grooming.

"It's just like people hair, really. In fact, my hair is just like Stinker's. Or worse, it's like my mom's."

"My mom is as bad at hair as your mom is at cooking. When I was little, everybody made fun of me. It was pretty awful. I had to learn how to do my hair myself. I checked out books, I studied magazines. I've even examined the hair of the people in front of me at the movies. I learned everything there was to know. If I didn't take care of it myself, it would look just like hers."

I was actually starting to feel bad for Angeline.

"But there was one kid in kindergarten," Angeline continued, "who didn't make fun of me." She pointed to the shot of Miss Bruntford as a kid on our project.

"Miss Bruntford?" I said.

Angeline pulled down the photo and handed it to me. "Yeah, right. I can't believe you let the joke go this long," she said. "I was sure you were going to crack."

I read the back of the picture. Written in clumsy kindergarten writing, it said, "To Annie from Jamie."

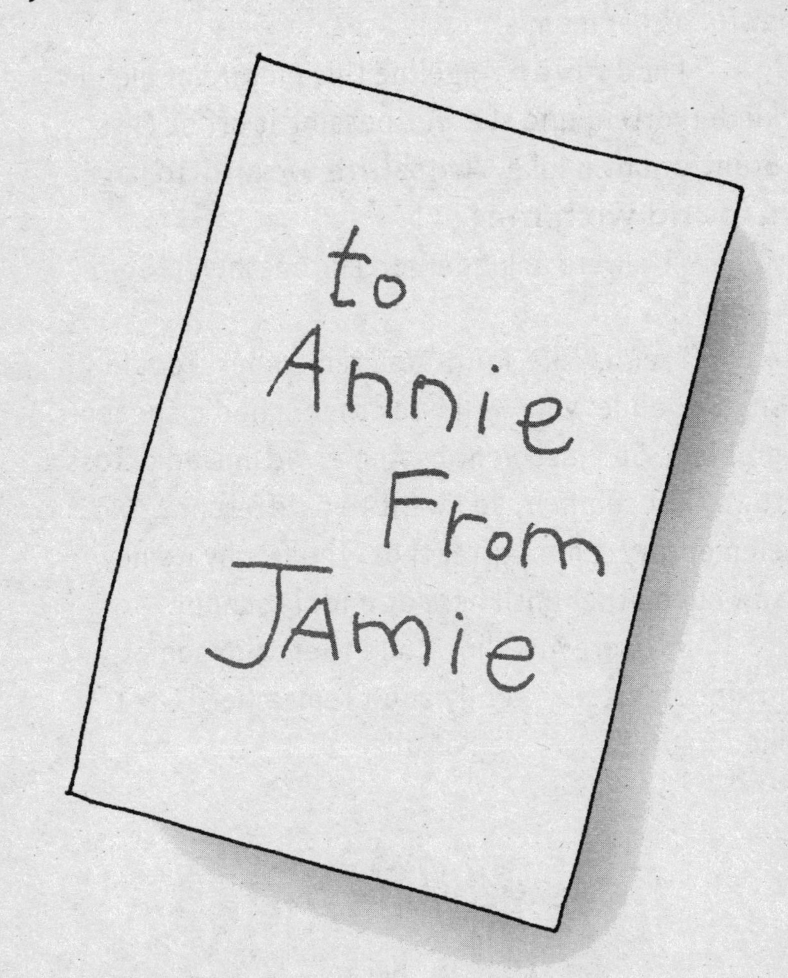

It was my handwriting. This wasn't a picture of Baby Bruntford. This was a picture of ME!!!!

Suddenly, Angeline's mom **DID** look a little familiar to me. Maybe I **had** seen her before. And way back then, Angeline's hair was, well, just as awful as her mom's.

I had **given** Angeline this picture of me in kindergarten, and she was passing it off as Miss Bruntford as a joke. ***Angeline* was kidding around with me!!!!**

"We were in kindergarten together," I said numbly.

"Yeah," she said. "You remember. I couldn't say 'Angeline' very well back then. I had a speech problem. So I just went by Annie. We moved across town that summer, so I went to a different elementary school after that. That's why we never saw each other until here at middle school."

So, were Angeline and I friends or something in kindergarten? I really can't remember kindergarten very well at all.

Angeline sat back down and started eating the meat loaf.

"You're eating my mom's meat loaf?" I asked her, and she pointed with her fork at Mom, who was sitting alone and dejected at a corner table, staring at piles and piles of her rejected steaming meat loaf.

I sat down and started eating it, too. I owed it to Mom. This meat loaf drove Stinker to Angeline, who gave him his makeover, and it drove the kids out of the lunchroom long enough for us to take down the Baby Bruntford photo.

It may be nauseating, but who else's mom's meat loaf can do all that?

MOM
Incredibly, even Angeline's gagging noises are kind of pretty.

The bell rang, and as we left the lunchroom, I put the awful picture of Stinker where the Baby Bruntford pic had been on our art project. Mom tried to look like she disapproved, but she was grateful.

It was a busy day, Dumb D, but since my fairy-tale report is due tomorrow, we'd better stop "chatting" now so I can get started on it.

Miss Bruntford
Then
Now
it made me wish that Stinker was even uglier.

Friday 27

Dear Dumb Diary,

Mr. Evans made me give my report first today, like he always does. I told him I had done my report on a few different fairy tales.

First, I talked about the witch in *Snow White,* and how she used a poison apple to make herself look better, but she could have just as easily used a poison meat loaf. Fairy tales remind us that there really are wicked, mean people walking around.

But fairy tales are short, and they leave out certain things, like, who do you think had to wash Rapunzel's hair after the Prince got his muddy boots all over it? That's right: Rapunzel did.

And you may think that these Princesses have it easy, but some of them started out as Ugly Ducklings, and some of the swans may actually end up as Ugly Ducklings. Fairies can do that to a swan, you know.

The ugly duckling that grew into an uglier duck.

And then I looked right at Isabella as I finished up my report, and I said that Hansel and Gretel made a mistake with the bread crumbs. They almost got eaten up because of it, but they stuck together and they got out of the woods in one piece. And Isabella knew what I meant.

But I had to admit, I'm not sure I ever really figured out *The Frog Prince.*

Mr. Evans throbbed only a little, which means I got a B. Isabella and I made up at lunch, which was good, since it looks like Mr. Prince is gone forever, now that Miss Bruntford is back. (I could just die!) I'm certain he'll write me when he settles in at his next job.

I admitted to Isabella that her kitten was the cutest pet in the photos, and she said that Stinker had never looked better.

I gotta admit- Isabella is awfully clever

I told her about Angeline. Isabella doesn't believe Angeline and I ever knew each other in kindergarten. Except last night after my report, I dug through my old school stuff and I found a picture. The writing on the back was unreadable, but I really think this may be Angeline.

FRONT
I think it's Kindergarten Angeline!
Here's what she wrote on the BACK

I told Angeline I was coming over to get Stinker tomorrow, and she said she'd do my hair if I wanted her to.

Think about it: **This is like having Einstein offer to help you with your math homework.**

or if my mom tutored you in the dark art of poisoning

OR if Mr. Prince taught how to be all totally handsome

(CYJD?)

or if any parent anywhere gave lessons on embarrassing kids.

Saturday 28

Dear Dumb Diary,

So I taped that kindergarten picture of Angeline into my diary and took it over to her house to ask if it was really her. She said it was, and was all excited that I keep a diary because she says she does, too.

I think I was surprised that
Angeline's house was NOT full of
the fanciful pink unicorns you
would probably expect.

But then she asked if she could read it.

Awkward, right? Since on one or two occasions, I may have written something unpleasant about Angeline, and I **REALLY** wanted her to fix my hair. So I said I'd let her read the love poems that Mr. Prince had sent me, but that was it.

Angeline looked a little startled, and read the first one and smiled. Then she read the second one and grinned.

"These aren't from Mr. Prince," she said.

"What makes you say that?" I asked, getting angry, but not angry enough to walk away from a hair makeover.

"I get a **lot** of notes, Jamie. I can identify

the handwriting of every boy in the school. These were written by Mike Pinsetti. See? M.P. doesn't stand for Mr. Prince, it stands for Mike Pinsetti."

For a moment, I thought I could taste yesterday's meat loaf.

"See, Pinsetti's nicknaming skill has two sides. He's also a good poet. He's just good with words in general."

Yup, it was yesterday's meat loaf all right.

"Also, Mr. Prince is dating Miss Anderson. At first, I'm sure he probably thought she was a bit old for him, but that picture of her in our art project may have changed his mind."

Curse those who can pose adorably!

"And by the way, Jamie, if you really do think that a teacher or any old guy has sent you a poem like this, he totally belongs in Gross Guy Prison. You're in **middle school.** Seriously. You should know better."

I didn't know what to say. Angeline was right. I weakly flipped to the third poem and, as Angeline read it, I saw her face totally change.

"Take your dog and go," she said. Just like that.

"Go?" I said.

"Go. No cutting. No styling. No highlighting. No moisturizing. No silkifying. No conditioning, and definitely NO ZONE SHAMPOOING!" She handed me Stinker and ushered us out the door, and I don't know which one of us was more upset about leaving.

"Angeline, why?" I said. "What did I do?"

"The poem," she said. "The lousy one. That's **Hudson's** handwriting. Do you honestly think I'm going to fix your hair and help you win Hudson back?"

And she slammed the door.

So there **IS** such a thing as **Zone Shampooing!** Can you imagine what I could have become?

Sunday 29

Dear Dumb Diary,

I spoke to Isabella on the phone this morning and she says that Angeline withholding her hair technology goes to show that maybe I *was* right before: Pretty Maidens **ARE** the cause of all the troubles in fairy tales. That, and jealousy.

Isabella told me that the reason she had gone through with the photo assignment is that she was jealous of me. Weeks ago, when I attempted my own version of Zone Shampooing on Hudson and was led away by Mr. Evans, I hadn't seen Hudson's reaction. Isabella saw **pure love** squirting out of Hudson's ears. Zone Shampooing had worked.

But not because I had fragranced him. Only Angeline could have taught me the right way to do that. But because Hudson thought I was **funny**.

Then when Isabella saw Pinsetti squirt pure love out of his ears, too, *and* she thought Mr. Prince was sending me poems, she couldn't help herself. Isabella turned into **The Evil Queen of Pure Jealous Revenge.**

After Isabella and I hung up, I tried to figure out the whole Frog Prince thing.

I was the frog for Mr. Prince, but he was the Prince for Miss Anderson. I was the frog for Hudson, then the Princess, and then the frog again. So it looks like I'm both the Princess *and* the frog.

Later on, the doorbell rang, and I found a letter on my front porch. I opened it and found this poem inside:

YOUR EYES

I saw your picture on the wall,
It seemed to hypnotize.
I saw the kind and gentle heart
Behind your big brown eyes.
M.P.

And then I knew that I really was the Princess. I was the Princess for Mike Pinsetti. Sure, it's only Pinsetti, but at least **I'M TOTALLY THE PRINCESS.**

But then I read the poem again. I don't have brown eyes. Nobody in my family has brown eyes.

When I flipped the envelope over, I saw it was addressed to Stinker. I guess the work Angeline did on Stinker moved Pinsetti to write a poem. Considering how ugly that little beagle began, I suppose he is the only **real** Frog Prince in this whole dumb fairy tale. And if I have to give up my throne to somebody he probably deserves it most of all.

Thanks for listening, Dumb Diary

Jamie Kelly

Think you can handle another Jamie Kelly diary? Then check out

Dear Dumb Diary,

Isabella said that she got the information about this charity online and I could help her collect for it if I wanted to, so as we made the rounds for the clothes, we also picked up a few bucks here and there for the Juvenile Optometry Federation.

Hooray! Now I have a charity to work for. In your face Angeline — now I'm as gentle and sweet as you, you pig!!

CAN'T GET ENOUGH OF JAMIE KELLY?

CHECK OUT HER OTHER

DEAR DUMB DIARY

BOOKS!

www.scholastic.com/deardumbdiary